Created, written, and drawn by
DONALD SIMPSON

Introduction by
AL FRANKEN

ibooks
New York
www.ibooks.net

DISTRIBUTED BY SIMON & SCHUSTER, INC.

A Publication of ibooks, inc.

Megaton Man ™ and
copyright © 2004 Donald Simpson
All rights reserved.

Originally published as
Megaton Man #1-5 by Kitchen Sink Press

Introduction copyright © 2004 by Al Franken

ibooks, inc.
24 West 25th Street
New York, NY 10010

The ibooks World Wide Web site Address is:
http://www.ibooksinc.com

The ibooks Graphic Novels Web site Address is:
http://www.komikwerks.com

ISBN: 0-7434-9758-9
First ibooks, inc. printing: December 2004
10 9 8 7 6 5 4 3 2 1

Special thanks to Denis Kitchen
and Brandon Diaz for their invaluable help.

Cover art by Donald Simpson

Printed in the U.S.A.

"HOW GREAT I AM TO WORK WITH"

by

AL FRANKEN

HI... IT'S ME, AL FRANKEN!

AND IT'S GREAT TO BE WRITING THIS *INTRODUCTION* TO "*CLASSIC MEGATON MAN VOLUME ONE*" BY *DON SIMPSON* --OR *WHATEVER* IT'S CALLED!

"I FIRST ENCOUNTERED THE ART OF *DON SIMPSON* WHILE WRITING MY BESTSELLER, "*LIES AND THE LYING LIARS WHO TELL THEM: A FAIR AND BALANCED LOOK AT THE RIGHT.*"

HOOBOY.!! SIX WEEKS TO DEADLINE--!

--AND MY "*SUPPLY SIDE JESUS*" CHAPTER WILL *ONLY* WORK IF I CAN FIND THE *PERFECT ILLUSTRATOR*!

BUT WHO?

"I HAD WRITTEN A *PARODY* OF THOSE JEHOVAH'S WITNESS *KID'S STORY-BOOKS* CALLED "*THE GOSPEL OF SUPPLY SIDE JESUS*" WHICH NEEDED THE RIGHT CARTOONIST... LUCKILY I WOULD BE SPEAKING AT THE ANNUAL *ASSOCIATION OF AMERICAN EDITORIAL CARTOONISTS* IN A FEW WEEKS, SO I ENLISTED CHAIRMAN *ROB ROGERS* TO HELP FIND SOMEBODY."

JEEZ, AL! EVERYBODY I KNOW IS GAINFULLY EMPLOYED!

BUT THERE IS **ONE** GUY WHO MIGHT DO IN A PINCH!

ROB KEPT FOISTING THIS *DON SIMPSON* ON ME ... I WASN'T SOLD ON HIS *ART*, BUT I WAS IN A *BIND*-- SO I EMAILED THE SCRIPT TO HIM TO SEE WHAT HE COULD DO.

HIS *BIG IDEA* WAS PUTTING *JESUS* IN AN *ARMANI SUIT*! --CHRIST!! NOT THE RIGHT *INSTINCTS* FOR *THIS* JOB !!

DESPITE MY *MISGIVINGS*, DON DID HIS THING AND I GUESS IT TURNED OUT *OKAY*,

AT LEAST MY WIFE *FRANNI* APPROVED!

SO THEN DON BEGGED ME TO LET HIM DRAW THE *VIETNAM CHAPTER*, "*CHICKENHAWKS: EPISODE ONE*" FEATURING SOME FIFTEEN POLITICAL FIGURES.

DON *ASSURED* ME THAT HE WAS A *MASTER OF CARICATURE*... BUT HE KEPT DRAWING *BUSH* WITH A *GILLIGAN HAT*, WHICH REALLY ANNOYED ME!

THANKS TO MY FEUD WITH *BILL O'REILLY* AND THE LAWSUIT WITH *FOX NEWS* OVER THE USE OF THE PHRASE "*FAIR AND BALANCED*" -- AND, I LIKE TO THINK, MY FUNNY *WRITING* --"*LIES AND THE LYING LIARS WHO TELL THEM: A FAIR AND BALANCED LOOK AT THE RIGHT*" SHOT TO #1 ON THE BESTSELLER LISTS!

AND, WITH A LITTLE *DIRECTION*, I DON'T SUPPOSE SIMPSON'S ART *HURT* THE BOOK *TOO BADLY!*

ONLY NOW, NOT A DAY GOES BY THAT I DON'T GET *SPAM* FROM DON WITH HIS *LATEST MILLION-DOLLAR IDEA* FOR A *NEW COLLABORATION!* -- SHEESH!

ANYWAY, I'M GLAD DON'S GOT THIS NEW *MEGATON MAN* CHARACTER TO PUT HIS *ENERGIES* INTO, AND I WISH HIM THE BEST OF *LUCK!* I'M GLAD TO HAVE BEEN AN *INFLUENCE!*

--SAY *WHAT?* THIS IS A *REPRINT?* IT'S ALL *OLD STUFF* FROM *TWENTY YEARS AGO?!* HUH!! *MEGATON MAN*... NEVER *HEARD* OF IT!!

OH, WELL, ENJOY THESE CLASSIC *MEGATON MAN* ADVENTURES FROM THE "*AL FRANKEN DECADE*" -- I KNOW I WILL!

Y'KNOW, AS SOON AS IT'S *PUBLISHED*, WHEN I GET MY *COMP COPIES*-- I'LL READ IT ON A *PLANE*, MAYBE...

THANKS, AL!

Dramatis Personae

PRESTON PERCY... PREPPY PRIVATE EYE, ADVENTURER, COPY BOY--- HE WAS MEGATON MAN'S BEST PAL.

PAMELA JOINTLY... VERTIGINOUS COLUMNIST FOR THE *MANHATTAN PROJECT*, SHE BOTH LOVED AND HATED THE *MAN OF MOLECULES.*

RUDY MAYO... THE CITY EDITOR, HE WATCHED AS A WORLD TREMBLED.

THE PRESIDENT OF THE UNITED STATES... DID EVEN **HE** HAVE THE POWER TO AVERT THE DISASTER SET IN MOTION?

THE PROFESSOR... WERE SOME COSMIC SECRETS BETTER LEFT UNKNOWN?

This collection is dedicated to Denis Kitchen, Dave Schreiner, Pete Poplaski, Ray Fehrenbach, Bill Poplaski and Holly Brooks—the folks who originally made it happen.

MED BY | EDITOR AND PUBLISHER | ART DIRECTOR | COLORIST | ADDITIONAL MATERIAL BY | ASSOCIATE EDITOR, FERNDALE

IAN GABEL · DENIS KITCHEN · PETER POPLASKI · RAY FEHRENBACH · MICHAEL KAZALEH · CAROL QUITMEYER

As we leave our *harrowing heroes*, let's focus our attention on a series of *bizarre crimes*, each committed by a *single, costumed figure!* Each more *daring* than the *last!*

All goes according to *plan!*

BLAPF!

The *authorities* and their *linear perceptions* are easy enough to *out mode!*

NITE-TELLER

$

You're very *right*, sir. The terminal *does* list you as *president* of our *corporation.* Here's the check for *one hundred billion dollars...* --*Doctor software!*

Soon, not even *megaton man* shall pose a threat to me!

This *doctor software* creep is running *amok* all over the country!

The *Manhattan Project*

Why hasn't *megaton man* gone *after* him?

And just *who* is megaton man? Is he part of the *arms* build-up or something?

What's his *secret identity?*

Trent, do *you* have any idea?

Shucks *no*, Pam!

ON SALE NOW!

ASK FOR IT BY NAME!

I SURE WISH I COULD TAKE ON DOCTOR SOFTWARE-- BUT YOU NEVER KNOW WHEN SOMEONE WILL FALL OUT OF A WINDOW OR SOMETHIN'...

I TRY TO DIG UP EVERY BIT OF DIRT ON MEGATON MAN POSSIBLE-- YET I OWE HIM SO MUCH! HE'S ALWAYS THERE WHEN I FALL OUT OF A WINDOW!

HE MUST HAVE A CRUSH ON ME!

HERE'S THE A.P. WIRES, GUYS! SAY, Ms. JOINTLY! LOOK OUT FOR THAT WINDOW--

GOSH, MR. PHLOOG! ACE COLUMNIST PAMELA JOINTLY HAS FALLEN OUT OF THE DOG-GONE WINDOW AGAIN! WHY DOES SHE DO THAT, HUH MR. PHLOOG?

BROOM CLOSET

OVERKILL!

BOOM!

SIGH.

DAMNED IF I CLEAN IT UP!

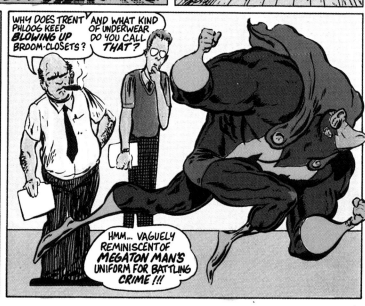

WHY DOES TRENT PHLOOG KEEP BLOWING UP BROOM-CLOSETS?

AND WHAT KIND OF UNDERWEAR DO YOU CALL THAT?

HMM... VAGUELY REMINISCENT OF MEGATON MAN'S UNIFORM FOR BATTLING CRIME!!!

WHAT THE---

ZOOM!

HEAT-GUIDED MISSILE! CAN'T SEEM TO SHAKE IT!

THAT MODERN *OFFICE COMPLEX* UP AHEAD!

--GIVES ME AN *IDEA!*

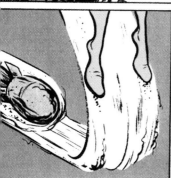

GOOD LORD!

A DOWNTOWN *SKYSCRAPER* WAS JUST *VAPORIZED!*

GOSH, CHIEF! WAS ANYONE INSIDE!?

NO, THANK GOD! IT WAS A *JOHN PORTMAN!*

ALL MY REPORTERS *MISSING* OR *KIDNAPPED* AND THE STORY OF THE *YEAR* EXPLODING OVER OUR HEADS! I'M GONNA COVER IT *MYSELF!*

PRESTON, THE MOST VITAL FUNCTIONS OF THIS *ORGAN* OF *FREE SPEECH* IS IN YOUR HANDS...

--INCLUDING THE *MOST* VITAL---

--THE *COMIC PAGE!* HMM... HERE'S THIS WEEK'S *DOOMESBURY'S*--

SATIRIZING THE CURRENT *CRISIS!*

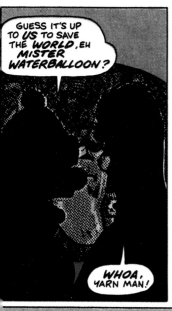

PRESTON PERCY, OLD MAN! HOW GOOD! TO SEE YOU!

GOSH, MR. PRESIDENT, IT'S GOOD TO SEE YOU TOO!

MEGATON MAN IS IN *TROUBLE*, SIR! IF HE GETS BEAT, THERE COULD BE A *WAR*!

THERE WON'T BE ANY *WAR*, MY YOUNG FRIEND!

BY THE WAY, HAVE YOU REGISTERED FOR THE *SELECTIVE SERVICE*?

GENTLEMEN! I HOPE I'M NOT ⸘AHEM⸘ *INTRUDING*!

PROFESSOR *LEVITCH*!

YOU'RE THE ONLY MAN *ALIVE* WHO CAN *HELP* US!

IT'S *MEGATON MAN* VS. *DOCTOR SOFTWARE* ---!

UH -- *YES*. ⸘AHEM⸘ I KNOW.

Er-- YOU SEE, *MEGATON MAN* IS MY OWN *CREATION*! AHEM---

---AND *DOCTOR SOFTWARE* IS MY --UH-- *TWIN* ⸘GULP⸘ *BROTHER*!

"**M**EGATON MAN WAS THE SOLE SURVIVOR OF A *DYING WORLD...*

OH NOO...

"THE INFANT ASTRONAUT WAS SUBJECTED TO MYSTERIOUS *CATACLYSMIC RAYS* - - -

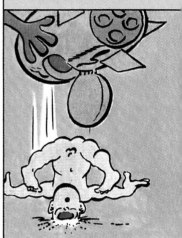

"HE WAS RAISED BY A LOST TRIBE OF *INTELLIGENT KANGAROOS...*

"AT A SCIENTOLOGY LECTURE, THE YOUTH WAS BITTEN BY A *RADIOACTIVE FROG...*

MAYONNAISE

"- - SUDDENLY, CAUGHT IN THE GRIPS OF A *SPACE-TIME CONTINUUM BLAST* - - -

"- HE SHOT A FURTIVE GLANCE ACROSS THE ROOM, THEN QUICKLY DOWNED THE *TOP SECRET PREMIUM SOLDIER SYRUP !!!*

"*THE UNTESTED GALACTIC ENERGY SURGED THROUGH HIS VEINS !!!* - -

SOMEHOW, HE FELT - - DIFFERENT !!!

PLEASE... NO MORE.....

" THUS WAS HE TRANSFORMED INTO THE MIGHTY *MAN OF MOLECULES - - MEGATON MAN!* "

SUDDENLY...

--THE CONTRAPTOID SPEWS FORTH TECHNOLOGICAL ADVANCEMENTS AND MAJOR INNOVATIONS...

WHERE'S MARSHALL McLUHAN WHEN I NEED HIM?

CAN'T HOLD OUT MUCH LONGER! POOR AUNT PETUNIA! HOW I'VE NEGLECTED HER--THE ONE WOMAN WHO RAISED ME!

OH, THAT TRENT!

Doomesbury
by M.F. Trombone

SID, HOW'S THE DEBACLE GOING?

PRETTY BAD, HOWIE! THE CONTRAPTOID'S STOMPING MEGATON MAN'S BUTT!

GOSH! 'S'ERE ANYTHING WE CAN DO?

JUST SAVE FACE WITH THE AMERICAN PEOPLE!

--ASK FOR MEGATON MAN'S RESIGNATION AND BUILD MORE MISSILES!

SO, MEGATON MAN IS OUT AND "MINUTE-MAN" IS IN?

YUP. ONE DENSE-PACK FOR ANOTHER!

YOU ARE DOOMED, MEGATON MAN! YOUR FATE IS SEALED!

PAMMY! NOW'S YOUR CHANCE! RUN, WHILE I'M DISTRACTING THEM!

BESIDES--

--WHEN I START BEATING THESE GUYS UP, IT ISN'T GOING TO BE PRETTY!

SHE'S OF NO FURTHER INTEREST TO ME! LET HER RUN! SHE WON'T GET FAR!

WHAT'S THAT SUPPOSED TO MEAN? HAVE YOU LAID SOME DEADLY TRAP FOR HER, FIEND?

NO. IT'S JUST THAT WE'RE ON TOP OF A SKYSCRAPER!

THERE GOES PAMELA JOINTLY-- MY ACE COLUMNIST!!! -- NO DOUBT CHASING AFTER ANOTHER STORY!

DAMN FINE REPORTER!

PAMMY! ≤SOB≥

DOES IT HAVE TO END THIS WAY? SO NEEDLESSLY?

IT COULD HAVE BEEN SO BEAUTIFUL --

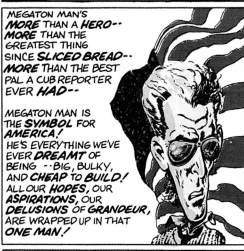

WE'RE TOO LATE.

DEATH BE NOT PROUD FOR YOU HAVE TAK A NO

SORT OF HATE TO SEE THE RIGHT-WING GOON GO--WHAT'LL I WRITE ABOUT NOW?

I WONDER WHO THAT UNSELFISH MAN BEHIND THE GOGGLES WAS! THAT SECRET HE'S TAKEN TO HIS DEATH!

AND WHAT OF THE CHILD IN MY WOMB? IS IT HIS? WILL REX EVER FIND OUT? WILL IT RUIN MY AIR HEADED LIFE?

FITTING HE SHOULD GO OUT IN A BLAZE OF GLORY, JUST LIKE THE LIFE HE LED, OWING ME FIFTY BUCKS!

THEN, I AM WITHOUT PEER! I AM RULER OF PLANET EARTH!

DON'T COUNT YOUR CHICKENS BEFORE YOUR BRIDGES ARE BURNED, SOFTWARE!

I'M LEAVING MEGATOWN FOR AWHILE -- THERE'S A FEW THINGS I'VE GOT TO THINK OVER.

SO HERE'S THE KEYS TO THE APARTMENT. DON'T LET THE PLANTS DIE WHILE I'M GONE, HUH?

SURE, BABE. TAKE CARE!

I DON'T KNOW HOW LONG I'LL BE GONE, BUT WHEN I RETURN, I WON'T BE FALLING OUT OF SKYSCRAPERS!

RIGHT ON, SISTER!

BYE, PAM!

GUESS SHE DIDN'T HEAR ME.

GASP!

AWE!

ASTONISHMENT!

--AND SO, LADIES AND GENTLEMEN OF THE PRESS...

--AS YOU CAN PLAINLY SEE... TRENT PHLOOG AND I ARE NOT ONE AND THE SAME!

HE'S RIGHT!

MEGATON MAN IS OVER THERE...

--AND HERE'S TRENT PHLOOG, SLUMPED OVER HIS DESK ALL DAY AS USUAL!

HIS SECRET IDENTITY SAFE ONCE MORE, MEGATON MAN GOES

ON PATROL!

"KEYS TO THE APARTMENT?"

NEXT: THE COSMIC CUE-BALL AND THE PARTYERS FROM MARS!

POP ART GALLERY!

THE DYNAMIC MEGATROPOLIS QUARTET!

I AM--THE *PEEPER!* IT IS *MINE*--TO *PEEP!* THAT IS, *OBSERVE* -- HOW DID THE *JUDGE* PUT IT? *"FORCEFUL ENTRY FOR PURPOSES OF PEEPING!"* --*WITLESS DOLTS,* SUCH AS *THESE!*

OKAY! DID ONE A YOUSE LEAVE THE *SCREEN DOOR OPEN* AGAIN?

BEHOLD THE *MEGATROPOLIS QUARTET!* CHUCK ROAST, THE *HUMAN MELTDOWN!* BING GLOOM, *YARN MAN!* AND REX RIGID, *LIQUID MAN!*

IS HE ONE A' YOUR FRIENDS?

YOU *CRUISIN'* FOR A *BRUISIN'?*

BEHOLD, THE *COSMIC CUE-BALL!* --SAFE FOR NOW, BUT *SOON* ---

IT WILL CAUSE *UNTOLD MAYHEM* --

NOW, *WAIT A MINUTE!* THAT'S *LIBEL!* THE *COSMIC CUE-BALL* IS *FOREVER SECURE* IN OUR *POSSESSION!*

YEAH! EVERYONE HERE TREATS IT WIT' DE *UTMOST CARE!*

METHINKS I SHALL *OBSERVE* A GM *BOARD MEETING INSTEAD!*

THUS SHALL I *CROSS-OVER* INTO THE *WALL STREET JOURNAL!*

--AND THEN ONTO THE *VILLAGE VOICE* FOR A *12-PART MAXI-SERIES* ---;*sigh* ---;

MEGATROPOLIS QUARTET OF *EARTH*-- HEED MY *WARNING!* IT SHALL COME TO PASS THAT YOU SHALL *RECRUIT A REPLACEMENT* TO YOUR RANKS WHO IS SO *MONUMENTALLY STUPID,* THAT THE *CUE-BALL* IS IN *DANGER OF ESCAPING!*

WHAT DID HE *MEAN,* RANKING OUR *RETENTIONS?*

HE'S GOT A *POINT!* WHO *WOULD* WE RECRUIT IF WE EVER NEEDED A *REPLACEMENT?*

WELL, *THAT WRAPS UP ANOTHER CASE*, EH, *MEGATON MAN*? WHAT, WITH *DOCTOR SOFTWARE* SAFELY BEHIND *BARS* AND THE DREAD *CONTRAPTOID* BLOWN TO *SMITHEREENS* IN THAT *EXPLOSION*!

"KEYS TO THE *APARTMENT*?"# #*LAST ISH.*

QUARTET, ASSEMBLE! I HAVE A *FATEFUL ANNOUNCEMENT!* WE'RE A *TRIO* NOW, AND *THAT* DOESN'T BEGIN WITH A *"Q"...*

DON'T EVEN *SAY* IT, *SQUISHO!* WE *READ* YA LOUD 'N *CLEAR!*

DIS MEANS...

NEXT: "THE END OF THE MEGATROPOLIS QUARTET!"

WELL, SO LONG, MEGATON MAN! WE GOTTA GET BACK TO THE *PAPER* AND SEARCH FOR A *NEW CONTROVERSIAL COLUMNIST!*

I'LL SAY HELLO TO YOUR *SECRET IDENTITY* FOR YOU WHEN I *SEE* HIM!

MEGATON MAN! WE IN *QUARTET-DOM* ARE IN DIRE NEED OF AN *AUXILIARY MEMBER* TEMPORARILY! WOULD YOU BE *AVAILABLE?*

PROFESSOR RIGID! YOU'RE ASKING ME TO JOIN THE *MEGATROPOLIS QUARTET?!!*

WELL, UH, JUST AS LONG AS IT'S *TEMPORARY*, SURE!

I MEAN, I CAN'T LET *YOU* GUYS DISBAND!

AFTER ALL, *DOCTOR SOFTWARE* IS SAFELY BEHIND *BARS*, AND THE DREAD *CONTRAPTOID* WAS BLOWN TO *SMITHEREENS* IN THAT *EXPLOSION!* THIS CASE IS ALL *WRAPPED UP!*

GOSH, PAM! I'VE HARDLY EVEN BEEN OUT OF THIS *CITY* BEFORE!

BUT, STELLA! SURELY YOU'VE BEEN AROUND THE *WORLD* WITH THE *MEGATROPOLIS QUARTET*, AVERTING *DISASTERS*, AVENGING *EVIL*, AND ALL THOSE FANTASTIC THINGS!

OH, SURE, *MONSTER ISLANDS*, *MUTANT REFUGES*, AND *PARALLEL DIMENSIONS*, IF THAT'S YOUR IDEA OF FUN!

HMMM... THAT *COULD* GET MONOTONOUS AFTER AWHILE!

--AND ALL WE EVER DID IN BETWEEN WAS SIT IN THAT SCREWY *TOWER*, IN THOSE SILLY SUITS, DRINKING *INSTANT COFFEE*!

I WANNA *BUY CLOTHES* FOR A CHANGE! *TRAVEL!* HAVE AN *EXCITING CAREER*, LIKE *YOU*!

WELL, THERE'S CERTAINLY NO ONE TO STOP YOU!

PAM, WHY'D YOU QUIT YOUR JOB? YOU WERE *FAMOUS*!

LIFE BACK THERE WAS--- GETTING *HECTIC*... HA! YOU'RE LEAVING MEGA-TOWN BECAUSE YOU HAVEN'T SEEN THE WORLD, *ME*, BECAUSE I'VE SEEN *TOO MUCH* OF IT!

ANYWAY, I'M REALLY LOOKING FORWARD TO *TEACHING* AND *LECTURING* AT MY OLD *ALMA MATER*, WORKING ON SOME *SERIOUS WRITING*, AND COOLING OUT FOR AWHILE! *SAY*, MAYBE YOU'LL WANT TO TAKE A FEW *CLASSES* WHILE YOU'RE THERE!

WOW! THE *IVY-COVERED HALLS* OF *HIGHER LEARNING*! AND ME, A *PARTYING UNDERGRAD*, WAITING TABLES IN A *RESTAURANT*, STUDYING ALL NIGHT, EACH DAY AN *EARTH-SHAKING STRUGGLE* TO MAKE THE GRADE!

AND IN THE TEEMING *MIDWEST*! I'LL *DO* IT!

I WISH I COULD SEE THE WORLD THROUGH *YOUR* EYES, STELLA! YOU MAKE THE ACADEMIC ROUTINE SOUND LIKE AN *AD-VENTURE*!

WHY, EVEN *PAYING* THE *RENT* COULD BE SOME SORT OF *EPIC BATTLE*!

WE GET TO *PAY* THE *RENT?* WOW!

OH, BROTHER!...

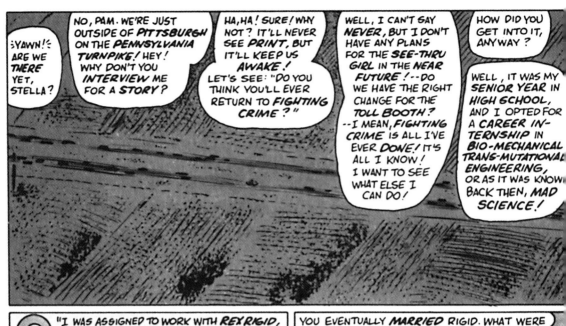

SYAWN! ARE WE *THERE* YET, STELLA?

NO, PAM. WE'RE JUST OUTSIDE OF *PITTSBURGH* ON THE *PENNSYLVANIA TURNPIKE!* HEY! WHY DON'T YOU *INTERVIEW* ME FOR A *STORY?*

HA, HA! SURE! WHY NOT? IT'LL NEVER SEE *PRINT,* BUT IT'LL KEEP US *AWAKE!* LET'S SEE: "DO YOU THINK YOU'LL EVER RETURN TO *FIGHTING CRIME?*"

WELL, I CAN'T SAY *NEVER,* BUT I DON'T HAVE ANY PLANS FOR THE *SEE-THRU GIRL* IN THE *NEAR FUTURE!* --DO WE HAVE THE RIGHT CHANGE FOR THE *TOLL BOOTH?* --I MEAN, *FIGHTING CRIME* IS ALL I'VE EVER *DONE!* IT'S ALL I KNOW! I WANT TO SEE WHAT ELSE I CAN DO!

HOW DID YOU GET INTO IT, ANYWAY?

WELL, IT WAS MY *SENIOR YEAR* IN HIGH SCHOOL, AND I OPTED FOR A *CAREER IN-TERNSHIP* IN *BIO-MECHANICAL TRANS-MUTATIONAL ENGINEERING,* OR AS IT WAS KNOWN BACK THEN, *MAD SCIENCE!*

"I WAS ASSIGNED TO WORK WITH *REX RIGID,* THE MOST BRILLIANT *EGG-HEAD* ON EARTH! I WAS HEAD OVER HEELS IN LOVE!

THE TECHNICAL TERM FOR THIS IS *CHEMICAL!*

CAN *YOU* SAY THAT?

GOSH!

"HE WAS NICE. HE MADE *DECISIONS* FOR ME. AND SOON, OF COURSE, WE WERE *COSMICALLY TRANS-FORMED* INTO THE *MEGATROPOLIS QUARTET!*"

YOU EVENTUALLY *MARRIED* RIGID. WHAT WERE YOUR *AGES,* YOU AND HE?

I WAS SEVENTEEN, HE WAS *SIXTY.*

SIXTY! MY *GOD!*

GENIUSES AREN'T *BORN,* THEY'RE *MADE!*

STILL, THAT'S *QUITE* AN *AGE DIFFERENCE!*

I GUESS IT WAS!

THAT TAKES CARE OF MY *NEXT* QUESTION: WHY YOU DIDN'T HAVE ANY *CHILDREN!*

MY READERS WILL WANT TO KNOW WHAT YOU DID WITHOUT A *SEX LIFE!*

I SHOULDN'T TELL, BUT... *OFF THE REC-ORD,* I *DIDN'T* DO WITHOUT. I SOUGHT THE COMPANY OF *OTHER HEROES,* SOME *VILLAINS... MACHO JERKS,* MOSTLY!

OBVIOUSLY, YOU WERE *DISCREET...*

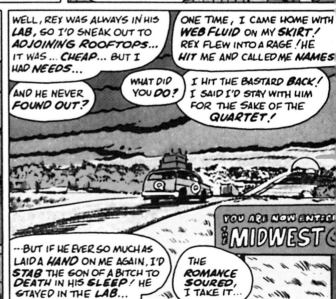

WELL, REX WAS ALWAYS IN HIS *LAB,* SO I'D SNEAK OUT TO *ADJOINING ROOFTOPS...* IT WAS ... *CHEAP...* BUT I HAD *NEEDS...*

AND HE NEVER *FOUND OUT?*

WHAT DID YOU *DO?*

ONE TIME, I CAME HOME WITH *WEB FLUID* ON MY *SKIRT!* REX FLEW INTO A RAGE! HE HIT ME AND CALLED ME *NAMES*

I HIT THE BASTARD *BACK!* I SAID I'D STAY WITH HIM FOR THE SAKE OF THE *QUARTET!*

--BUT IF HE EVER SO MUCH AS LAID A *HAND* ON ME AGAIN, I'D *STAB* THE SON OF A BITCH TO *DEATH* IN HIS *SLEEP!* HE STAYED IN THE *LAB...*

THE *ROMANCE* SOURED, I TAKE IT...

YOU ARE NOW ENTER[...] *MIDWEST [...]*

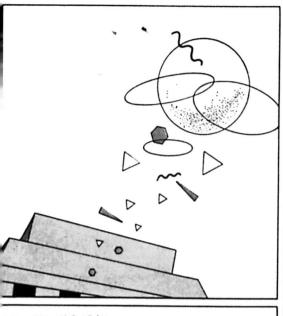

THAT WAS NO ORDINARY CUE-BALL...

ORDINARY ?!!! YOU IDIOT !!! THAT WAS THE

COSMIC CUE-BALL!

THE COSMIC CUE-BALL!

THE BILLIARD OF GREAT POWER! THERE'S NO TIME TO LOSE! QUARTET, ASSEMBLE!

STEADY, REX.

HOLD ON, MEGS. YOU'RE NEW HERE. WE'VE BEEN THROUGH THIS A THOUSAND TIMES! LET ME EXPLAIN QUARTET PROCEDURE.

SEE, THE CUE-BALL ESCAPES, IT FALLS INTO THE HANDS OF SOME SUPER-VILLAIN, SAID VILLAIN IS ELEVATED TO GODHOOD, SAID GODHOOD PROCEEDS TO MAKE A BID FOR WORLD DOMINATION, WE BUST 'IM, AND THE CUEBALL IS RETURNED TO ITS CONTAINMENT UNIT. AND BELIEVE ME, IT'S POINTLESS TO SEARCH FOR IT NOW.

BESIDES, RIGHT NOW WE HAVE A SEVERE RODENT PROBLEM!

THE *MEGATROPOLIS QUARTET* -- *REBORN!* DOES THIS MEAN THEY'VE BECOME *RELIGIOUS* ? -- *MEGATON MAN* -- NOW KNOWN AS *CAPTAIN MEGATON MAN!* DOES THIS SIGNIFY AMERICA'S INCREASED *MILITARISM* ? THE *COSMIC CUE-BALL* -- *BACK IN THIS DIMENSION* BY *POPULAR DEMAND!* -- BUT WHEN WILL IT *STRIKE* ? AND, OF ALL THINGS, *ENTER* -- THE *MEGATON MICE.!!!* WITHOUT OUR *CONTROVERSIAL COLUMNIST*, WE HAVE NO MEANS TO *INTERPRET* THESE EVENTS! WE'RE A SHIP WITHOUT A *RUDDER!* WHAT A CRUMMY TIME FOR *PAMELA JOINTLY* TO GO OFF AND *FIND HERSELF.!!!*

Manhattan Project

NOT TO MENTION, CIRCULATION IS *DROPPING!* DEMOGRAPHICS ARE *SHIFTING!* *FREE SPEECH* ALONE JUST DOESN'T SELL NEWSPAPERS!

The Manhattan Project
PARTYERS FROM MARS!

ABOUT THE MOST CONTROVERSIAL THING IN THE *PROJECT* THESE DAYS ARE THE *FUNNIES* ...!!!

DOONESBURY©

SIR, WE'VE PUT SOME "WORST-CASE" SCENARIOS TOGETHER! IF THE SOVIETS FIND THE CUE-BALL, WE MAY AS WELL SURRENDER!

GASP!

--IF SOME WHACKY TERROR-IST GROUP GETS IT, WE'RE ALL GONERS!

GOOD LORD! CHOKE!

--AND IF THE OTHER PARTY GETS IT DURING YOUR RE-ELECTION BID...

(TURNS BLUE)

by M.F. TROMBONE ©

SHALL WE SEND MEGATON MAN AFTER IT ?

WHAT ?!! THE EIGHT-BALL AFTER THE CUE-BALL ?!!

M.F. TROMBONE

BLEEDER BAILE

NANCY THE NAZI

BUT OF *COURSE!* M.F. TROMBONE IS THE MOST *INFLUENTIAL* MAN IN *AMERICA!* I BET HE'D *JUMP* AT THE CHANCE TO WRITE A *COLUMN* OF COMMENTARY! GIVE HIM A CALL!

MAYNARD F. TROMBONE, PLEASE! THIS IS AN EMERGENCY!

PRESTON! HOW YA DOIN', OLD PAL! SAY *WHAT* ?

BUT *PRES!* DO YOU KNOW HOW MUCH RE-SEARCH A COLUMN LIKE *PAMMY'S* TAKES ?

NO KIDDING! A TON!

AND DO YOU KNOW HOW MUCH RESEARCH A STRIP LIKE *MINE* TAKES ?

THAT'S *RIGHT!* NEXT TO *NONE!*

NO DICE! HE SAYS HE'S ENSCONCED IN HIS MEDIUM!

Diary - 8/10
Just a brief note —
Settled in on campus
— 2 bedroom apt on
S University Ave —
— start classes in a
week —

Stella found job at Burger King — Now she's registering for classes! I think we should get along rather well — although I worry —

She's used to having someone make descisions for her: its hard not to play "Big Sister" to her. There's a lot of risky stuff a naive girl like her can get

into in this town — but a lot of good experiences, too. She's got to find things out for herself — / Meeting with the old gang tonight — sigh —

YOU'RE DECLARING YOUR *MAJOR* AS *LIBERAL ARTS*, IS THAT RIGHT?

YES!

WELL, HERE ARE ALL YOUR *PUNCHCARDS, GUIDEBOOKS,* & STUDENT I.D!

YOU'RE NOW ENROLLED IN THE *IVY-COVERED HALLS OF HIGHER LEARNING!*

CONGRATULATIONS! YOU REALIZE, OF COURSE, THAT YOU'LL BE PAYING $640,000 FOR A PIECE OF PAPER THAT'LL BE *ABSOLUTELY WORTHLESS* IN TODAY'S JOB MARKET!

BUT DAMN IT, I ADMIRE YOU! IT TAKES GUTS TO TAKE THE TOUGH ROUTE! YOU THINK FOR YOURSELF

I'VE BEEN THINKING FOR MYSELF FOR *TWENTY-FOUR HOURS!*

IT'S NOT SO *TOUGH!*

JEAN-LUC GODARD FILM FESTIVAL
5 BIG OBSCURE CLASSICS!

GEE! THIS WAS MY FIRST ENCOUNTER WITH FOREIGN CINEMA! THERE'S A LOT OF STUFF I DIDN'T UNDERSTAND!

LIKE, WHY DIDN'T JEAN-PAUL BELMONDO JUST BLAST THE BAD GUYS WITH COSMIC BOLTS? WHY DIDN'T ANNA KARINA USE HER ELEMENTAL POWERS AGAINST EDDIE CONSTANTINE? WHY DID JEAN-PIERRE LÉAUDE JUST LET CHANTAL GOYA WALK ALL OVER HIM INSTEAD OF FLAMING ON?

YOU MEAN, INSTEAD OF DEALING WITH THEIR ALIENATION ON A HUMAN LEVEL, TRYING TO ALTER THEIR ENVIRONMENTS EMOTIONALLY AND INTELLECTUALLY--

--THEY SHOULD JUST WREAK MAYHEM? WHAT A HEAVY, BEAUTIFUL CONCEPT!

SURE! IT WORKS, TOO!

WOW! I CAN'T WAIT 'TIL I TAKE YOU TO YOUR FIRST FELLINI FESTIVAL!

I'M ALMOST AN INTELLECT ALREADY!

A TOAST TO PAMELA JOINTLY -- WHO LEFT AND BECAME WORLD FAMOUS -- AND HAS NOW RETURNED TO OUR GROUP!

IT'S GREAT TO BE BACK!

I HEAR YOUR ROOMMATE IS A SUPERHERO! ISN'T THERE A DANGER OF RADIATION POISONING?

SAY, WHERE'S PRESTON? I HAVEN'T SEEN HIM SINCE YOU'VE BEEN BACK.

HE DIDN'T COME WITH ME.

HE STAYED IN NEW YORK. MEGATON MAN WAS ALWAYS HIS HERO, YOU KNOW. ANY-WAY, IT WAS OVER BETWEEN US.

MISS JOINTLY!

HI! I'M TAKING YOUR LECTURE COURSE THIS SEMESTER! SAY, DIDN'T YOU USETA FALL OUT OF SKYSCRAPERS OR SOMETHIN'?

I'VE RETIRED.

I *DON'T* BELIEVE IT!

I BELIEVE IT!

YARN MAN'S HIT THE *SACK*, THE *HUMAN MELTDOWN* AND *FELICIA* ARE DELVING INTO *AESTHETICS*...

I'LL SEE IF *RIGID* IS STILL UP! I GOTTA DISCUSS THIS *COSTUME*...

REX, THIS MOLECULARLY UNSTABLE CIRCUITRY IS... *GROWING!*

DON'T TOUCH! IT'S *GOOD* FOR YOU!

IF YOU *SAY* SO...

LISTEN! DO YOU *HEAR* THAT?

IT'S THE *KID*-- AND *FELICIA*~

ER,... *PAINTING*...

GIGGLE! SQUEAKING BED SPRINGS

PAINTING, INDEED! YOU *CLOD!* THEY'RE HAVING *SEX!*

SEX! THAT DISTASTEFUL *ORGANIC* PROCESS! YOU KNOW WHAT IT *DOES*, DON'T YOU? IT INTERFERES WITH *SCIENTIFIC RESEARCH!*

SHOULD BE *OUTLAWED!*

NO *WONDER* STELLA LEFT YOU, REX! YOU'RE -- *PECULIAR!*

SINCE WHEN ARE YOU AN *EXPERT...*

ON *OTHER* PEOPLES WIVES!

COULD IT BE SINCE *YOU* AND *STELLA* HAD A *BRIEF, TORRID LOVE AFFAIR* BEHIND MY *LAB-COATED* BACK?

YOU *KNEW* ABOUT ME AND STELLA? EVEN *BEFORE* YOU ASKED ME TO JOIN THE *MEGATROPOLIS QUARTET?* BUT *WHY?*

WHY ALL THE *RIGOROUS TESTING?* WHY THIS NEW, UNTESTED *COSTUME?* WHY THAT *GUN...?.....*

WHAT ON EARTH ARE YOU DOING?

LEAVE THOSE CIRCUITS *ALONE!* THOSE *POOR* CIRCUITS NEVER HURT ANYONE! STOP! *STOP!*

--TOO LATE! YOU'VE *KILLED* THEM ALL... YOUR *HEAT SHIELD-ING...* YOUR *FORCE FIELD...* YOUR *AIR CONDITIONING...* ...SNIFF!...

YOU HAVE MURDERED INNOCENT WIRING! THIS IS NOT A PROUD THING, MEGATON MAN!

BUT THEN--? WHY--?

--THE *GUN*, MEGATON MAN? NOT KILL YOU, YOU *DIMWIT!* --I SIMPLY SPOTTED OUR *LITTLE FRIENDS...*

WHAT THE HELL ARE YOU JUST *LAYING* THERE FOR? WHAT IF THOSE HOODS KILL YOUR *UNCLE BING?*

I'M NO *COP!* IT'S NOT *MY* JOB!

SURE, I KNEW, ABOUT YOU AND *OTHERS!* I DIDN'T *CARE...* I JUST WANTED HER TO BE THERE...TO HOLD MY HAND...I WANTED *SO* FOR THIS LIFE TO *APPEAL* TO HER... I JUST WANT HER *BACK...*

YES, BUT *MINE* AREN'T! THEY MAY BE *TEAMING UP* TO *DESCEND UPON US* EVEN AS WE *SPEAK!*

MISTER METAFYZIK, THE CLAW, DOCTOR DEMISE, THE ARMS OF KRUPP, THE OLD SCOUT, MISTER BRAINDEAD... ANY *ONE* OF THEM IS A TOUGH CUSTOMER...

--AND THEY'RE ALL OVERDUE FOR A *BID* AT *WORLD DOMINATION!* --IF THEY'VE SOMEHOW *JOINED FORCES...*

WE'VE BEEN *THINKING,* MEGATON MAN! MAYBE YOU'D BE *HAPPIER ELSEWHERE!*

YOU DON'T REALLY NEED US!

SHE'S RIGHT, YOU KNOW! THE *MEGATROPOLIS QUARTET* IS JUST *HOLDING* YOU *BACK!!!*

OH *NO!*

IT'S TOO LATE!

26

"THE END OF THE MEGATROPOLIS QUARTET!"

GOSH, MEGATO... I MEAN, *MR. PHLOOG!* CIRCULATION IS *DROPPING!* DEMOGRAPHICS ARE *SHIFTING!* IF WE DON'T FIND A *CONTROVERSIAL COLUMNIST* SOON, WE'LL ALL BE LOOKING FOR *WORK!* --SPEAKING OF WHICH, HERE'S TODAY'S *ASSIGNMENT!*

--ALTHOUGH I SEE YOU HAVEN'T MADE MUCH PROGRESS ON *LAST MONTH'S!*

YOU KNOW, TRENT PHLOOG IS A REAL NICE GUY, BUT HE REALLY LACKS *INITIATIVE!*

TRENT PHLOOG!

HUH? WHA--? I'M SORRY!!!

TRENT! THE MANHATTAN PROJECT FACES A *CRISIS!*

CRISIS? WHO DO I LOOK LIKE! MEGATON MAN?

I NEED A TEMPORARY *CONTROVERSIAL COLUMNIST!* CAN YOU BE A *LIBERAL MUCKRAKER* ON A *DAILY BASIS?*

MR. MAYO I CAN'T EVEN SAY IT!--

--BUT--JUST AS ONG AS IT'S EMPORARY-- URE! I MEAN, CAN'T LET THE ROJECT GO UNDER, CAN I ?

SUPER!

NO-- MEGATON!

PRESTON PERCY, BRING THE *PAMELA JOINTLY* CLIPPINGS!

NEXT ISSUE:

"ROCKETS & LOVE!"

MEGATON MAN is ON PATROL!

MEGATROPOLIS! A MODERN-DAY *KINGDOM* OF GRANITE AND GIRDER! THE BIGGEST *CITY* IN THE *WORLD!* BIGGER THAN ALL *GET OUT!* JUST *HUGE!* AND *AMERICAN,* FRIEND! *AMERICAN* WITH A *CAPITAL "A"!*

ATOP THE *TOWERING SKYSCRAPERS,* A *LONE FIGURE* STANDS, KEEPING *VIGIL,* GUARDING THE *FREE WORLD*-- EVER AT THE *READY* SHOULD SOME *BAD GUY* TRY TO *SCREW* WITH *DEMOCRACY!* HE SPEAKS----

AMERICA IS *BACK!* WE'RE *STRONG* AGAIN! AND MORE *SECURE* THAN *EVER!*

--AROUND ME IS THE *EVIDENCE!* *BUILDINGS* FULL OF *PEOPLE*-- COLLATING *INFORMATION* TO COMMUNICATE TO *OTHER PEOPLE*-- IN *OTHER* BUILDINGS!

MY HEART *POUNDS!*

OVER *THERE*-- AMERICAN *FACTORIES* CHURNING OUT AMERICAN *PRODUCT* FOR THE *TEEMING MASSES!*

IT BRINGS *TEARS* TO MY *EYES*--- AND *BUILD-UP* TO MY *GOGGLES!*

AND DOWN *THERE!* AMERICAN *FREEWAYS*-- CLOGGED WITH AMERICAN *TRAFFIC!* THE *ARTERIES* OF *WESTERN CAPITALISM!*

AND ONLY *NOW,* AFTER *TWO WEEKS,* DO THE NEW *ROADS* AND NEW *CARS* SHOW ANY SIGN OF *FALLING APART!*

I AM *WELL PLEASED!*

HMMM... *CIVILIZATION* IS AWFULLY *QUIET* TODAY-- *TOO* QUIET! I SENSE A *SAGA* ABOUT TO *UNFOLD* -- SOME UNFORESEEN *DRAMATIC CATALYST* DISTURBING THIS SERENE *TABLEAU*-- SPARKING *CONFLICT* AND *CHARACTER DEVELOPMENT!*

IS IT AN *EARTHLING?*

GOOD VS. *EVIL* IN *EARTHSHAKING CONFLICT!* POETIC *MOMENTS!* *PATHOS!* AND *PLOT CONSTRUCTION* WHEREIN WE LEARN A LITTLE *MORE* ABOUT *OURSELVES!*

NO! IT'S A *MOUNTAIN* IN A *CLOWN SUIT!*

SHALL WE ENDEAVOR TO MAKE AN *ENCOUNTER?*

WELL, I *STAND*-- AT THE *READY!*

NEGATIVE! IT IS NOT YET *TIME* FOR THE CHOSEN HOUR OF *CONTACT!*

FIRST-- WE MAKE A *BEER RUN!!!*

FIN.

Art, Script and Lettering: Donald Simpson ...... Editor and Publisher: Denis Kitchen ..... Front Cover Color: Peter Poplaski ..... Color (pages 1, 8-32): Ray Fehrenbach ..... Color (pages 2-7, back cover): Bill Poplaski

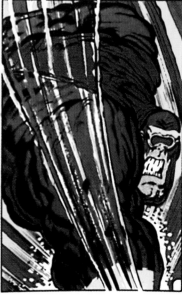

IF ANYONE SHOULD *ASK*, I'M TAKING *INVENTORY* OF THE AMMONIA...

TRENT PHLOOG!

WOO!

TRENT PHLOOG!

WHERE THE HECK IS *TRENT PHLOOG?*

UH, *HERE* I AM, MR. MAYO, SIR!

I WAS JUST, UH--TAKING *INVENTORY...*

I'M *WAITING*, PHLOOG.

HERE I COME, MR. MAYO, SIR! I WAS JUST-- *AMMONIA--*

NEED ME TO *LIGHT* YOUR CIGAR, MR. MAYO, SIR?

NO, TRENT. THIS MORNING, I LIT *THIS* ONE BY MYSELF.

TRENT, THIS GREAT NEWS-PAPER FACES A *CRISIS* LIKE NONE ITS EVER *SEEN!*

BUT ALL I DID WAS-- *DON'T HIT!*

TRENT, CAN YOU BE A *LIBERAL MUCK-RAKER* ON A *DAILY BASIS?*

BUT I WAS JUST-- AMMONIA-- *WHAT?*

WOO! WHAT YOU *SAID!*

TRENT, HAVE A SEAT. LET ME EX-PLAIN THE POSITION I'M IN.

EVER SINCE PAMELA JOINTLY'S DEPARTURE, THE *PROJECT'S* BEEN WITHOUT A *CONTROVERSIAL COLUMNIST.*

CIRCULATION HAS SLIPPED BAD-LY-- OUR *MARKET SHARE* IS DWINDLING-- *DEMOGRAPHICS* HAVE SHIFTED. I'VE SEARCHED HIGH AND LOW FOR A *TEMPORARY REPLACEMENT.*

TRENT, YOU'RE MY *LAST HOPE!*

ME? A COLUMNIST? WELL, AS LONG AS IT'S *TEMPORARY!*

GREAT! THESE ARE CLIPPINGS OF PAMELA JOINTLY'S PULITZER PRIZE-WINNING CONTROVERSIAL COLUMNS! NOW, JUST READ THESE, PICK UP ON THE *STYLE*, THE *TONE*, THE *ATTITUDE* OF HER WRITING! TAKE THE REST OF THE *MORNING* IF YOU NEED TO!

COLUMNIST TRENT PHLOOOGG

THEN, WRITE ME A SERIES OF COLUMNS *JUST LIKE THESE!*

I NEED THE FIRST ONE BY 5!

AND TRENT, *THANKS.*

MEGATON MAN: FLUNKY FOR THE PENTAGON?

SAY, PRESTON! I JUST REALIZED, I NEVER REALLY READ ANY OF PAMMY'S COLUMNS! HA HA

I DON'T GET IT.

WHAT THE HELL *ARE* THEY?

OH, YOU KNOW, *SCREEDS* AND *DIATRIBES* AGAINST THE *ARMS RACE, SEXISM, RACISM*, YOU KNOW, *LIBERAL CAUSES* --

LIKE *BANNING MEGATON MAN!*

WHY? YOU GETTING SECOND THOUGHTS?

WHY-- *NO*, I... WAS JUST CONCERNED THAT I'D HAVE TO *COMPROMISE*...

MY INTEGRITY...

NT. PHL'OOG

DROP IN! TURN ON! BLAST OFF! BURN OUT! GO WEST, YOUNG JOURNALIST, AND THROW UP WITH THE COUNTRY! DO YOUR OWN THING! GET IT TOGETHER! YOU CAN RUN, BUT YOU CAN'T *HIDE*...

SN'T THAT WHAT PAMMY SED TO SAY?

CHIEF, NO ONE'S TALKED LIKE THAT FOR A GOOD FIFTEEN YEARS!

YOU OLD SOFTY! YOU'RE WORRIED ABOUT HER!

I MISS HER. IT MAY SURPRISE YOU, BUT I VALUED HER AS A HUMAN BEING.

THE QUESTION IS, WHY ARE YOU TAKING THIS SO CALM? SHE WAS YOUR GIRLFRIEND!

DO YOU SUPPOSE SHE'S MADE THE RIGHT DECISION -- FOR HERSELF?

PAMMY KNOWS WHAT SHE'S DOING, CHIEF.

WHAT AM I DOING?

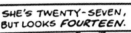

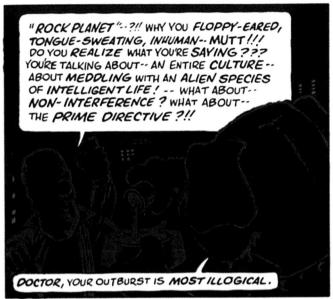

"ROCK PLANET" --?!! WHY YOU FLOPPY-EARED, TONGUE-SWEATING, INHUMAN-- MUTT!!! DO YOU REALIZE WHAT YOU'RE SAYING??? YOU'RE TALKING ABOUT-- AN ENTIRE CULTURE-- ABOUT MEDDLING WITH AN ALIEN SPECIES OF INTELLIGENT LIFE! -- WHAT ABOUT-- NON-INTERFERENCE? WHAT ABOUT-- THE PRIME DIRECTIVE?!!

DOCTOR, YOUR OUTBURST IS MOST ILLOGICAL.

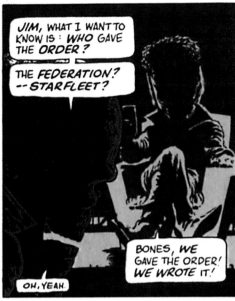

JIM, WHAT I WANT TO KNOW IS: WHO GAVE THE ORDER?

THE FEDERATION? --STARFLEET?

BONES, WE GAVE THE ORDER! WE WROTE IT!

OH, YEAH.

HEY, WE'RE PARTYERS FROM MARS, REMEMBER? WE'RE ANARCHISTS! WE RECOGNIZE NO AUTHORITY-- SAVE OUR OWN! THERE IS NO FLEET BUT THIS SAUCER!

AND DON'T SPILL ANYTHING, GANG! MY DAD'LL KILL ME!

CAPTAIN, A PARTY OF THAT MAGNITUDE WOULD ENTAIL THE ENLISTMENT OF GLOBAL TELECOMMUNICATIONS, TYING THE ENTIRE PLANET INTO A MASSIVE, TACTILE MEDIA EVENT.

BURP.

THE OPPORTUNITY TO PARTY WITH EVERY SINGLE BEING ON THE PLANET.!!! MEDIA OFFICER, WHO IS THE MOST INFLUENTIAL EARTHLING ON EARTH?

CAPTAIN, I HAVE EXAMINED THE ARTIFACT AND HAVE IDENTIFIED THE ONE WE SEEK!

WHO? THE PRESIDENT? MEGATON MAN? YARN MAN? PAMELA JOINTLY?

CUST...

BY M. F. TROMBONE

The Manhattan Project

DOOMESBURY

OUTRAGEOUS PREMISE!

TOPICAL SET-UP!

"HIP COLLOQUIALISM!"

SITUTIONAL BUILD-UP!

"SNIDE COMMENT!"

SNAPPY, ABSURD COMEBACK!

PUNCH LINE!

PATENTED ODDLESS BURPE RECOIL REMARK!

"NEAR FUTURE?"

I'M YARN MAN! I'M A CITIZEN OF THE DISTANT FUTURE!

WELL, THAT'S CERTAINLY ENCOURAGING.

THE NAME'S RECKLESS. ROGER RECKLESS. TECHNOLOGIST BY TRADE! YOU'VE MET JEANIE...

TECHNOLOGIST? GEE! COULD YOU RETURN ME TO THE PRESENT?

SORRY, MY SPECIALTY WAS MILITARY! YOU KNOW, BUILD 'EM, AIM 'EM, KEEP THOSE SILOS OILED! SURE DID THE TRICK, Eh?

SORRY 'BOUT THAT BLAST, THOUGH. LOOKS LIKE YOU CAUGHT THE BRUNT OF IT! BUT THEY'RE DOING MARVELOUS THINGS WITH PLASTIC SURGERY THESE DAYS!

IT'S EASY TO BLAME THE TECHNOLOGISTS, THOUGH. BUT HEY! WE JUST MAKE THE STUFF TO BE AS DEVASTATING AS POSSIBLE! WE DON'T GIVE THE ORDERS FOR THE DESTRUCTION OF CIVILIZATION, Y'SEE. NO INDEPENDENT THOUGHT ENTERS INTO IT AT ALL!

BLAME THE POLITICIANS. WE WERE JUST DOING OUR JOB!

I DON'T BLAME YOU....

YOU'RE A GOOD SPORT, I CAN SEE THAT!

'COURSE, IF WE HAD KNOWN THEY WERE REALLY WHACKY ENOUGH TO PUSH THE BUTTON-- HA HA (IT KILLS ME) I GUESS WE WOULDN'T HAVE BUILT 'EM AS ACCURATE OR AS DEADLY!

WHY, HELL, WE MIGHT'VE DONE SOMETHING TO PREVENT DOOMSDAY! BUT, LIVE AND LEARN, I ALWAYS SAY!

THE SHOE'S ON THE OTHER FOOT NOW, RIGHT?

GOD! I CAN'T STAND LOOKING AT YOUR DISFIGUREMENT!

PROFESSOR! COME QUICKLY! THE TRANSPORT OUT OF THIS SECTOR IS HERE!

WE HAVEN'T MUCH TIME...

★FINAL
SCIENTISTS
SPECULATE:
GIANT
CATS IN
FUTURE?
YARNMAN IN DANGER?
WILL MEGATON
MAN ATTEMPT
DARING RESCUE?

AHEM. THERE IS NOTHING OF *JOURNALISTIC INTEREST* IN THE *BROOM CLOSET,* MEGATON MA- --er, Mr. *PHLOOG!*

YOU WEREN'T THINKING OF MAKING ANY DARING *RESCUE ATTEMPTS* BY ANY CHANCE?

WHY, *NO!* I WAS JUST...

HELLO! THIS IS WASHINGTON D.C.!

NO RESCUE?

SOME FRIEND YOU TURN OUT TO BE...

HELLO? WHO'S THERE?

WHY, POOR *YARN MAN* COULD BE *DYING...*

GET THE HELL OUT' MY *BROOM CLOSET,* THE *BOTH A' YOUSE!*

WELL, *TIME FOR LUNCH...*

OH, *NO* YOU DON'T! I'M *BUYING!!!*

YEAH, WE *LIVED* TOGETHER, WE HAD THE *HOTS* FOR EACH OTHER! BUT, *CAREERS CONFLICTED, PASSIONS COOLED!* ANYWAY, IT'S OVER.

LET'S *TABLE* IT, HUH?

SURE! WHATEVER YOU MRHMPHHSHMPH.!!!

OKAY! OKAY ALREADY! I'LL TELL YOU THE *FULL*, *STICKY* DETAILS OF *PAMMY* & *PRESTON*!

YOU *DO* WANT TO HEAR THE FULL, STICKY DETAILS, DO YOU NOT?

I'M A *LITERAL RUGMAKER*. I *TRAFFIC* IN STICKY DETAILS. *LET 'ER RIP.*

WE MET AT THE IVY-COVERED HALLS OF HIGHER LEARNING, HER, A *POLITICAL SCIENCE* AND *JOURNALISM* DOUBLE-MAJOR HONOR STUDENT, AND ME, A PREPPY PRIVATE-EYE AND CAMPUS LOAFER. THIS WAS THE MID-SEVENTIES, MIND YOU, AND THE SIXTIES HADN'T COMPLETELY DIED OUT -- TERRY KATH WAS STILL AROUND, AND SO FORTH.

WE SORT OF CONGREGATED AROUND THE BROWN JUG, A GROUP OF US (AMONG SUCH NOTABLES WAS THE YOUNG M.F. TROMBONE, THE CARTOONIST). ANYHOW ANN ARBOR WAS JUST A GREAT PLACE TO FALL IN LOVE WITH A SEXY, INTELLEC-TUAL BRUNETTE -- WE SHMOOZED IN THE CAFÉS, RENDEZ-VOUSED IN UNDERGRAD-UATE LIBRARIES, SAW CONCERTS AND FOREIGN MOVIES. I RECALL ON THE DIAG, IN THE MIDDLE OF CAMPUS, KISSING HER COLLAR-BONES -- sigh.

SHE DIDN'T SHARE MY TASTE FOR FRANK TASHLIN, BUT SHE DID ENJOY AN OCCA-SIONAL BOB CLAMPETT *TWEETY* AND *SYLVESTER*.

SHE BEGAN AS THE PERFECT STUDENT, BUT SOON BECAME DISENCHANTED, FRUSTRATED, SICK OF THE IVORY TOWER MENTALITY, THE HYPOTHETICAL ASSIGN-MENTS, THE ARBITRARY CURRICULUM. SHE YEARNED TO BE TESTED IN THE REAL WORLD. SHE'D HAVE NO MORE TO DO WITH SCHOOL OR GRADES OR SUCH.

MAYBE I HAD SOMETHING TO DO WITH THAT ATTITUDE. I LIKE TO THINK I PUT SOME INTRIGUE INTO HER LIFE. ME, I SORT OF LIKE THE BIZARRENESS OF THE CAMPUS SETTING, THE IDEA OF NEVER DOING ANYTHING WITH MY LIFE BUT BEING A PROFESSIONAL STUDENT.

SHE LEFT FOR NEW YORK. IT HAD BEEN A SWELL ROMANCE.

ONE PROBLEM, THOUGH. I MISSED HER. MY LIFE WAS EMPTY WITHOUT HER-- ANN ARBOR, A HOLLOW GHOST TOWN.

I FOLLOWED HER.

THE ONLY JOB I WAS QUALIFIED FOR WAS THAT OF COPYBOY AT THE SAME PAPER WHERE SHE WAS EMPLOYED. BUT I HAD TO BE NEAR HER.

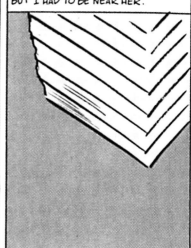

OF COURSE, DURING THE TIME WE WERE APART, THE JERKS AROUND THE OFFICE HAD BEEN HITTING ON HER, BUT SHE KNEW HOW TO TAKE CARE OF HERSELF!

MR. MAYO! TRENT PHLOOG IS SEXUALLY HARASSING ME!

NOT AGAIN.

PHLOOG, KNOCK IT OFF OR YOU'RE FIRED!!!

BUT-- NO ONE AT THE PROJECT KNEW YOU WERE LOVERS···

WE TRIED TO KEEP IT COOL IN THE HOPES OF SEPARAT- ING OUR CA- REERS AND PERSONAL LIVES.

BUT ULTIMATELY, IT WOULDN'T MATTER. THE PRESSURE STARTED BUILDING, IMPERCEPTIBLY AT FIRST. DOMESTIC LIFE BECAME A DRAG...

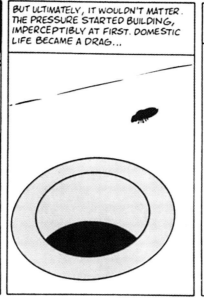

AND AT WORK, PAMMY GOT HER OWN COLUMN, WRITING WITTY ANECDOTES AND AMUSING PAP FOR THE MASSES.

"Pap Populi"
by

HER OWN BYLINE! IT WAS MORE THAN MY FRAGILE MALE EGO COULD HANDLE. THEN, ONE DAY...

MY GOD!!! YOU PUSHED HER TO HER DEATH!

NO, BUT THE THOUGHT HAD CROSSED MY MIND! BUT OF ALL THE CRUMMY LUCK, A NEW CRIMEFIGHTER EMERGED...

SUDDENLY, MEGATON MAN AND PAMELA JOINTLY WERE THE STORY OF THE YEAR. IT WAS WORSE THAN BEFORE...

SHE FINALLY FOUND A FOCUS FOR HER ENERGIES... SHE BECAME OBSESSED WITH HIM, AND MORE AND MORE FAMOUS!

SHE CHRONICLED -- AND CRITICIZED -- HIS EVERY MOVE, BATTLING THE CRIMSON MOJO, THE LEATHER NUN, THE ELECTRIC LIGHT ORCHESTRA, AND EVEN THE ORIGINAL BAD GUY!

SHE WON A PULITZER PRIZE AT THE AGE OF TWENTY-FIVE, AND I WAS STILL A...

BUT Y'KNOW, IF SHE'D ONLY HAVE APPRECIATED WHAT I GAVE UP TO BE WITH HER...

MAYBE WE HAD NEVER BEEN AS IN LOVE AS I THOUGHT... MAYBE SHE'D RATHER I'D NEVER FOLLOWED HER FROM ANN ARBOR... FUNNY, HER THERE NOW AND ME HERE...

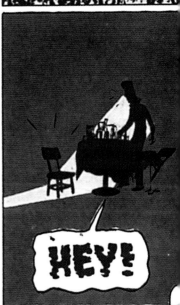

HEY!

THAT'S SOME MEAN FLYIN', KAT! WHERE'D YOU LEARN TO PILOT SMALL SPACE-CRAFT LIKE THAT?

ON THE STREETS, KID! NOW GO MEND MY FRIEND AN' MAYBE I'LL LETCHA *POLISH* MY BUTTONS!

SAY, WHAT'S OUR *DESTINATION?*

THE *NEXT* MORNING, BACK IN THE *PRESENT*...

I SEARCHED ALL OVER THE CITY! I DON'T KNOW HOW, BUT I *LOST* HIM! I GUESS THERE'S NO *COLUMN*, AND THE PAPER'S GONNA GO OUTTA *BUSINESS*...

AU *CONTRAIRE*, PRESTON! MEGATON MAN DROPPED OFF PHLOOG'S COLUMN YESTERDAY AFTERNOON, AND IT'S A *DOOZIE*!

MEGATON MAN?

PHONES ARE RINGING OFF THE *HOOK*! CIRCULATION'S GONE *THROUGH* THE *ROOF*! IT'S THE *CONTROVERSIAL EVENT* OF THE *DECADE*!

I WONDER WHY YOU NEVER SEE TRENT PHLOOG AND MEGATON MAN *TOGETHER*!

I'VE WONDERED ABOUT THEIR CONNECTION MYSELF! BUT AFTER *THIS* COLUMN, I DOUBT THE TWO WILL EVEN BE ON *SPEAKING TERMS*!

SAY! THIS IS PRETTY *OUTRAGEOUS STUFF*!

HEY! PBS WANTS YOU TO HOST A WEEKLY NEWS SHOW!

YOU'RE PRETTY *HOT*, BIG FELLA! GUESS I HAD YOU FIGURED *WRONG*!

WELL, PRESTON, IT'S ALL IN A DAY'S *CHARADE*-- I MEAN, *WORK*!

HAVE YOU *READ* THE ARTICLE YET?

WHY NO, I JUST GLANCED...

GQ WANTS A LAYOUT FOR THEIR SPRING ISSUE!

WILL MEGATON MAN SPARK WWIII?

WELL! TAKE A LOOK!

TRENT! YOU'VE JUST WON THE *PULITZER PRIZE*!!!

The Manhattan P

WILL MEG MAN SPA WWII?

BAD GUY PAROLLED FROM BIG HOUSE

by TRENT

NEXT: NEWS OF THE WORLD

the Manhattan Project #

WILL RUSSIA BUILD TH
MEGATON MAN
by Pame

NEWS OF THE WORLD

DONALD
SIMPSON
'85

Megaton Man Four

LET'S CHECK INTO THE *MANHATTAN PROJECT* AND SEE WHAT OUR HERO IS UP TO...

GOOD MORNING, MEGATON MA-- I MEAN, MR. PHLOOG!

WHOOPIE.

HERE'S THE A.P. WIRES, GUYS! ... *PARTYERS FROM MARS* HAVE BEEN REPORTED FREQUENTING *CONVENIENCE STORES,* PURCHASING LARGE QUANTITIES OF *BEER*....

...SCIENTISTS FEEL THAT THEY MAY BE AN INTELLIGENT LIFE-FORM, AS THEY ONLY CONSUME *IMPORTED BRANDS*...

..."*BAD GUY*" HAS BEEN PAROLED FROM JAIL, AND VOWS TO HUNT DOWN MEGATON MAN, WHICH SHOULD BE EASY, HE SAYS, AND I QUOTE:

"BECAUSE EVERYONE KNOWS THAT MEGATON MAN IS REALLY *TRENT PHLOOG*."

...BASEBALL COMMISSIONER *BARRY MANILOW* SAID TODAY...

I AM *NOT* TRENT PHLOOG!!!

SO LET'S DROP IT!

... I MEAN, UH, I'M NOT ... *MEGATON MAN*...

AHEM...

I SAY, OLD BOY, QUICK! WHAT'S THAT WORD THAT MEANS "TO DESTROY WITH AN EXCESS OF FIREPOWER"?

YOU MEAN, "OVERKILL"?

AH, PRECISELY!

BOOM

WOO!

...SUPPOSEDLY THAT'S MEGATON MAN'S *MAGIC WORD*... THANKS, OLD BOY!

"SUPPOSEDLY THAT'S MEGATON MAN'S MAGIC WORD!" FEH!

TRENT, YOU'RE THE MOST TALKED-ABOUT JOURNALIST OF OUR *TIME!* YOUR SCATHING ATTACKS ON *MEGATON MAN* AND THE *ARMS RACE* HAVE WON YOU THE *PULITZER PRIZE!* THE *MANHATTAN PROJECT* IS BECOMING MORE WIDELY RESPECTED THAN THE *NEW YORK TIMES* OR THE *WASHINGTON POST!* AND YOU'VE ONLY WRITTEN *ONE COLUMN!!!* AND TO THINK, ALL THIS TIME, MANY OF US AT THE PROJECT THOUGHT THAT *YOU* WERE REALLY *MEGATON MAN!* CAN YOU IMAGINE THAT?

BUT SIR, I REALLY *AM* MEGATON MAN! SOMEONE IN *WASHINGTON* WRITES THE COLUMNS *FOR ME* IN ORDER TO KEEP MY *IDENTITY SECRET!*

HA HA! YOU NUT YOU! I DON'T KNOW WHY I DIDN'T PROMOTE YOU *SOONER!* BUT SERIOUSLY, STARTING TOMORROW NIGHT, YOU'RE REPLACING THE *MACNEIL /LEHRER NEWS HOUR.* IT REALLY WON'T BE THAT MUCH EXTRA WORK. ALL YOU HAVE TO DO IS READ FROM YOUR *COLUMNS...*

OH, BUT THAT'S OUT OF THE QUESTION, SIR! YOU SEE, I'M NOT ALLOWED TO READ THEM. THEY'RE AFRAID I'LL *WISE UP* AND START *THINKING* FOR *MYSELF* OR SOMETHING!

HA HA HA HA HA HA, HA! A BRILLIANT SENSE OF HUMOR, REALLY! I'M GLAD TO SEE ALL THIS FAME HASN'T GONE TO YOUR HEAD! AS FOR *TOPICS,* HOW ABOUT A PIECE ON MEGATON MAN'S ABILITY TO INVADE THE PRIVACY OF AMERICAN CITIZENS? THE *INFRINGEMENT* OF THE *INDIVIDUAL'S RIGHTS?* THE *EROSION* OF OUR *PRECIOUS FREEDOM!*

GOODNESS! I WASN'T AWARE OF *THIS* DEVELOPMENT! IT'S AN *OUTRAGE!* I'M *APPALLED!* HOW DOES HE DO IT, PRAY TELL?

YOU KNOW, WITH THOSE WHACKY GOGGLES OF HIS! WHAT THEY CALL HIS *MEGATON VISION!!!* KINDA *SCARY,* ISN'T IT?

UH, *MEGATON VISION,* SIR?

MR. MAYO! MAY I SPEAK TO YOU?

WHAT IS IT, PETER PARKINGLOT, YOU INGRATEFUL STUDENT FREELANCE PHOTOGRAPHER, YOU? MORE PICTURES OF WALL MAN?

PAMMY BABY! SHAKE THAT THING! YOU ARE LOOKIN' GOO-OOD!!!

GLUTTINUS ONLY STAYS FOR COCKTAILS. PLANET EARTH SPARED!

WHY YES! HOW DID YOU KNOW?

BECAUSE, PARKINGLOT, YOU ALWAYS BRING ME PICTURES OF WALL MAN!

FOR GOD'S SAKE TRENT GROW UP

BUT I THOUGHT...

WALL MAN, WALL MAN, WALL MAN! YOU'RE A ONE-NOTE PHOTO-JOURNALIST!

PAMMY! IS IT SOME-THING I SAID?

AT LEAST HAVE THE DECENCY TO READ MY NEWSPAPER, IF ONLY TO SEE WHAT I MIGHT BE IN THE MARKET FOR, BEFORE YOU COME WALTZING IN HERE FIVE TIMES A DAY, TRYING TO SELL ME STUFF I CAN'T USE!

TSK!

the Manhattan Project

WILL RUSSIA BUILD THEIR OWN MEGATON MAN?

WHERE HAVE YOU BEEN, ANYWAY? MEGATON MAN SELLS PAPERS THESE DAYS! I NEED PICTURES OF MEGATON MAN!...FIGHTING CRIME, BLOWING HIS NOSE, WIPING HIS...

AFTER DECADES OF CAREFUL SELF-PRO-MOTION, MY ALTER EGO, WALL MAN, HAS BEEN PUSHED OFF THE FRONT PAGE. WHAT WENT WRONG? HOW COULD HE LOSE HIS MASS-APPEAL?

WALL MAN WILL GET TO THE BOTTOM OF THIS!

ARE YOU KIDDIN'? SHE WRITES ABOUT YOU ALL THE TIME! SHE HATES YOUR GUTS! SHE'S BIG NOSED AND FLAT CHESTED -- WHAT DO YOU SEE IN HER?

IF ONLY YOU COULD SEE HER THROUGH MY EYES...

OH, THE OL' MEGATON VISION, EH?

SHE HAS GREAT LEGS, I'LL ADMIT...

OH, WALLY,,, MAY I CALL YOU WALLY?... SHE'S SMART, INDEPENDENT, STRONG... SHE HAS CHARACTER... SHE THINKS FOR HERSELF,... NOTHING LIKE THE SEE THRU-GIRL, WHO WANTS THE GUY TO DO ALL THE THINKING, ALL THE PROBLEM SOLVING... LIKE HE WAS MEGA-TON MAN OR SOMETHING... WHO COULD LIVE UP TO THAT? WHO COULD TAKE THAT KIND OF DEPENDENCY?

THE SEE-THRU-GIRL! NOW SHE'S PRIME! THERE'S YOUR KIND OF WOMAN! WHY NOT GO AFTER HER..?

AS A MATTER OF FACT, SHE ASKED ME TO GO ON PATROL WITH HER...

I TOLD HER NO...

NO?!!! SHE WANTS YOU! GO FOR IT!!!

SHE HAPPENS TO BE MARRIED...

TO THAT OLD FART, PHIL FLACCID OR WHATEVER? WHO CARES?

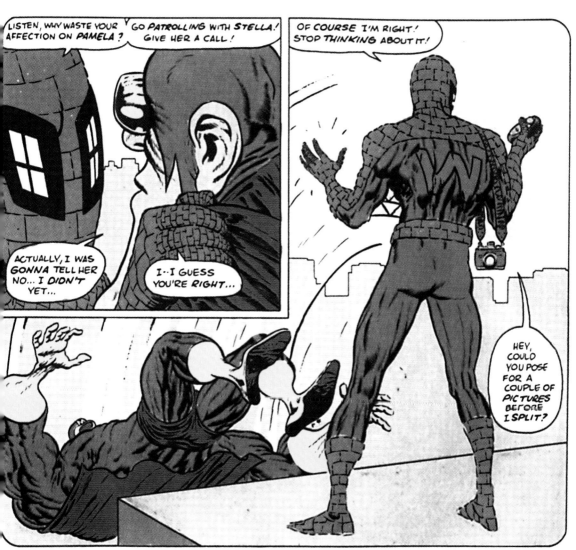

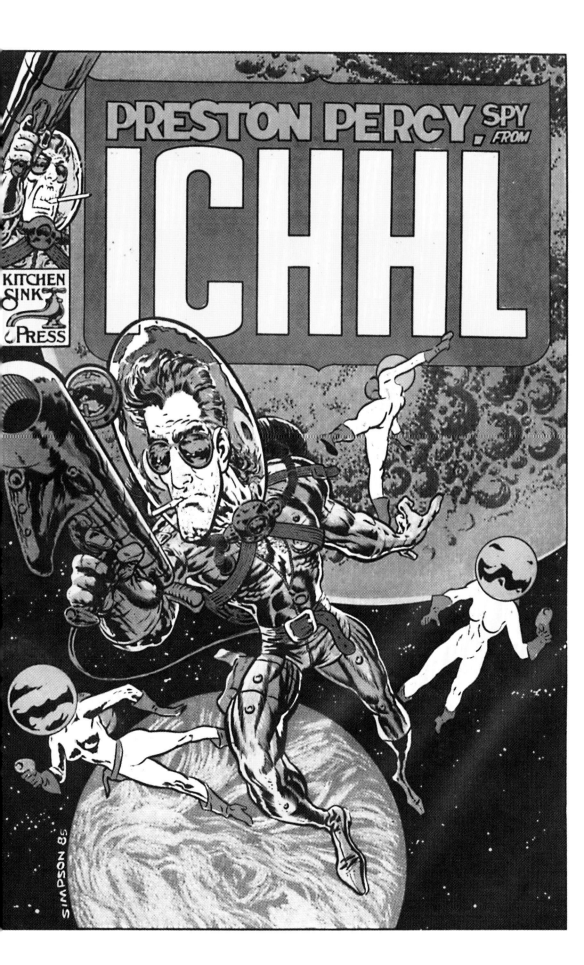

IN AN ORBITING AMERICAN PEACE-KEEPING *KILLER SATELLITE*, HE STANDS... A LONE, *BROODING* FIGURE.

TAKE A *GOOD, LONG LOOK* AT HIM, AMERICA...

...HE MAY WELL BE THE ONLY THING STANDING BETWEEN *YOU* AND *INTERNATIONAL ANARCHY*...

FOR, GENTLE READER, ONLY *THIS MAN* HAS *EYES* WILLING TO SEE... THE *WORLD* AS IT *TRULY IS.*

ONLY *HE* HAS A *CLEAR PICTURE*, FROM HIS *CELESTIAL VANTAGE POINT*, OF THE *ROT*, THE *SCUM*, THE *FILTH*... THAT ENCROACHES ON OUR *NATIONAL BORDERS*.

HIS *EYES*, VETERANS OF *TEN AMERICAN WARS*, MISS ABSOLUTELY *NOTHING.*

WHETHER IT'S A *COMMIE COFFEE-BEAN PICKER* IN *NICARAGUA*, OR A U.S. COLLEGE KID BUMMING A *STUDENT LOAN*...

...IT'S NOT GOING TO SLIP BY HIM AND HIS *KILLER SATELLITE* TO HARM THE LAND HE LOVES.

NO EVIL ESCAPES HIS SIGHT.

LIEUTENANT, YOU CALLED ME UP HERE TO *BRIEF* ME ON EVENTS THAT MAY *THREATEN* OUR NATIONAL SECURITY! MY TIME IS QUITE VALUABLE...

OF COURSE! THE *BRIEFING!* LET'S PROCEED DIRECTLY TO THE ALL-IMPORTANT BRIEFING, SECRET AGENT PERCY!

'I THINK YOU AGGRAVATED AN OLD *WAR WOUND!*

AGENT PERCY, YOU'RE THE ONLY MAN FOR THE JOB! SCANT MOMENTS AGO, MY HAND-PICKED CREW OF INTELLIGENCE PERSONNEL AND THIS KILLER SATELLITE'S SOPHISTICATED EQUIPMENT DETECTED THESE THREE CRISIS SPOTS WHICH DEMAND OUR IMMEDIATE ATTENTION---

HMM... LOOKS AS IF THE COSMIC CUE-BALL IS LOOSE AGAIN, A *SAUCER* FROM MARS HAS BEEN SIGHTED, AND YARN MAN AND *KOZMIK KAT* ARE MAROONED IN THE *FUTURE!*

BRILLIANT ANALYSIS! AND IT ALL HAPPENED IN THE LAST *HALF HOUR!*

LAST HALF HOUR, HUH? WELL I'LL *BE!* AND YOU AND YOUR EQUIPMENT *JUST* DETECTED IT, AND DECIDED TO GIVE ME A CALL! IMPRESSIVE!

GLAD TO SEE *ICHHL'S* ON OUR SIDE, RIGHT ON TOP OF THINGS!

THE *ASSOCIATED PRESS* WIRED THE STORY TO EVERY FARM-TOWN NEWSPAPER IN THE COUNTRY *TEN FULL WEEKS* AGO, BUT *THEY* SOMEHOW FORGOT TO *CALL* ME AND WASTE MY VALUABLE TIME!

STERANKOVICH, WHAT HAVE YOU AND YOUR *HAND-PICKED CREW* BEEN DOING FOR THE LAST *TEN FULL...*

..WEEKS..?

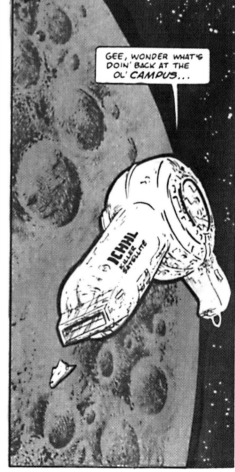

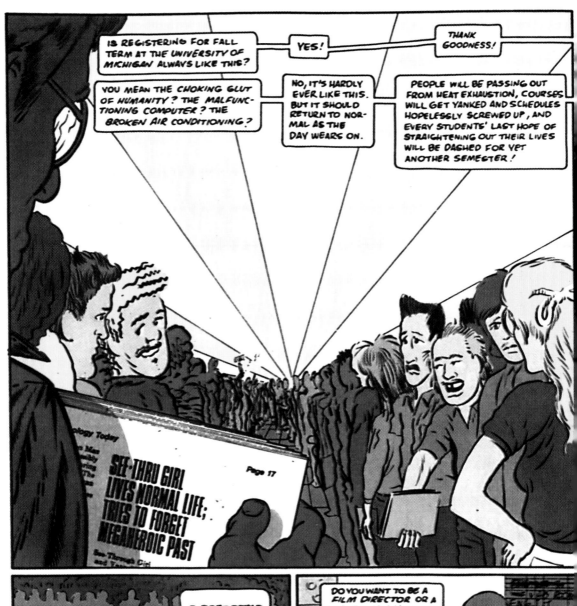

WELL GEE, WHEN DOES THE FUN BEGIN?

WITH FOOTBALL, OF COURSE!

SO WHICH DORM ARE YOU IN?

I'VE GOT AN APARTMENT A FEW BLOCKS FROM DOWNTOWN.

AREN'T YOU LUCKY! I GOT STUCK IN SOUTHQUAD ON THE TENTH FLOOR.

GREAT SCHOOL, MICHIGAN. BOYS AND STUFF.

YOU'LL BE COMPETITION IN THAT DEPARTMENT... BUT AS I WAS SAYING, THE WORST THING IS THE FIRE ALARMS GOING OFF AT FOUR IN THE MORNING. IT'S ALWAYS SOME JERK THEY CAN'T CATCH.

ENG. 406 BARTON

BUT STILL, YOU HAVE TO WAIT TWENTY MINUTES TO USE THE STAIRS FROM THE TENTH FLOOR AND WAIT OUTSIDE IN YOUR PAJAMAS FOR A HALF HOUR.

I SHOULD REMARK AT THIS JUNCTURE THAT THEY SHUT DOWN THE ELEVATORS FOR SAFETY REASONS, AND THE WHOLE AFFAIR TAKES 90 MINUTES WHILE EVERYONE CAN SEE YOUR PANTIES AND COLD CREAM! BUT YOU KNOW WHAT'S REALLY SCARY IS THAT THE CITY OF ANN ARBOR FIRE DEPT. ONLY HAS FIRELADDERS THAT CAN REACH THE EIGHTH FLOOR OR SOMETHING! SO WHAT HAPPENS IF THERE IS AN ACTUAL FIRE?

CRAWL DOWN THE WALLS!

CRAWL THE WALLS--? WHAT KIND OF---? WEIRD!

FIGHT CRIME?!!!

AW, GEE, STELLA, YOU'RE A SWELL KID AN' I'M REALLY FLATTERED 'N EVERYTHING BUT Y'KNOW, THERE'S SOMEONE ELSE AN' I JUST DON'T FEEL RIGHT ABOUT Y'NO...

JUST NOT FAIR TO EITHER OF US... FEELS... RIGHT, Y'NO... AND... WH...

NEXT: GEORGE HAS A GUN

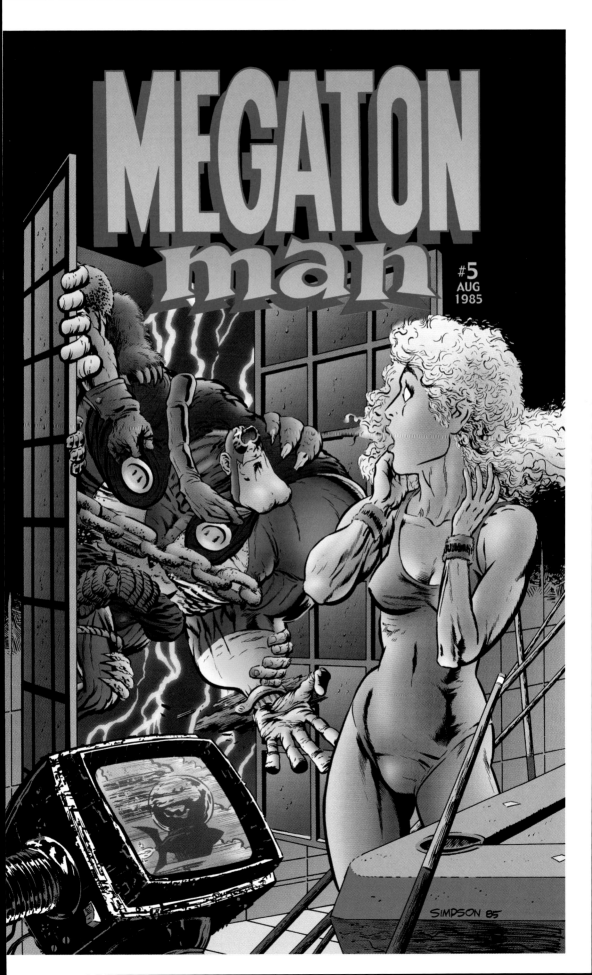

Stella's Story
Dramatis Personae

STELLA STARLIGHT...
SHE GAVE THE BEST YEARS OF HER LIFE TO DULL, MONOTONOUS CRIME-FIGHTING... AND THEN... WELL, CAN A *SEE-THRU GIRL* HELP IT?

REX RIGID...
BETRAYED BY HIS YOUNG WIFE AND THE BEST GUY ON THE PLANET... WAS *LIQUID MAN* ALL WASHED UP?

MEGATON MAN...
HE HAD STELLA, YET HE LONGED FOR PAMMY, HIS MOST VOCAL CRITIC. A REAL CLASS-A DOPE.

GEORGE HAS A GUN...
THE SAUCER OF THE ERST-WHILE *PARTYERS FROM MARS*... WILL THEY SAVE MANKIND, OR *DESTROY* IT?

RAY FEHRENBACH
COLOR ARTIST

BILL POPLASKI
COLOR ARTIST

DAVE SCHREINER
EDITOR

HOLLY BROOKS
CIRCULATION

PETE POPLASKI
COVER COLOR ARTIST

DENIS KITCHEN
PUBLISHER

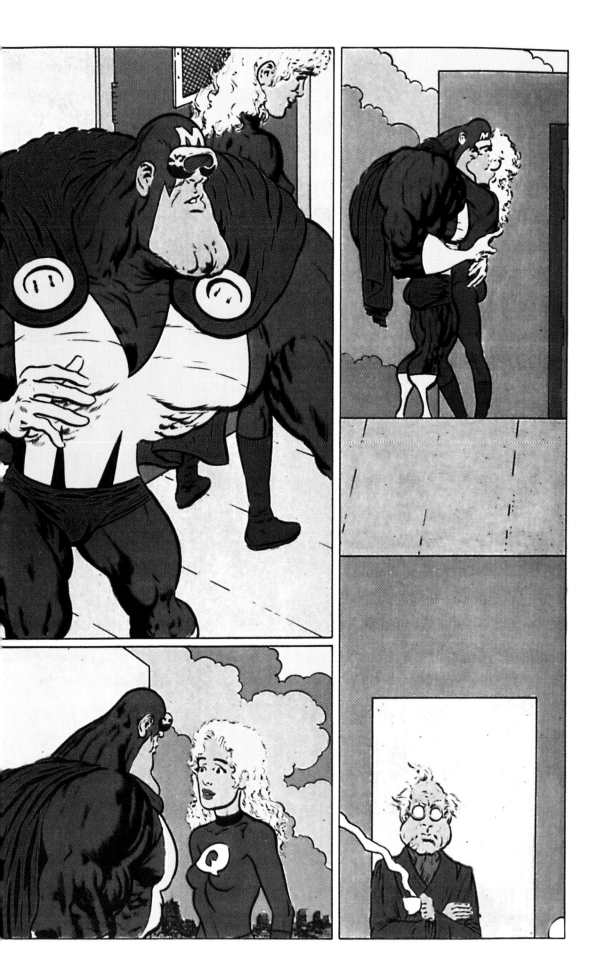

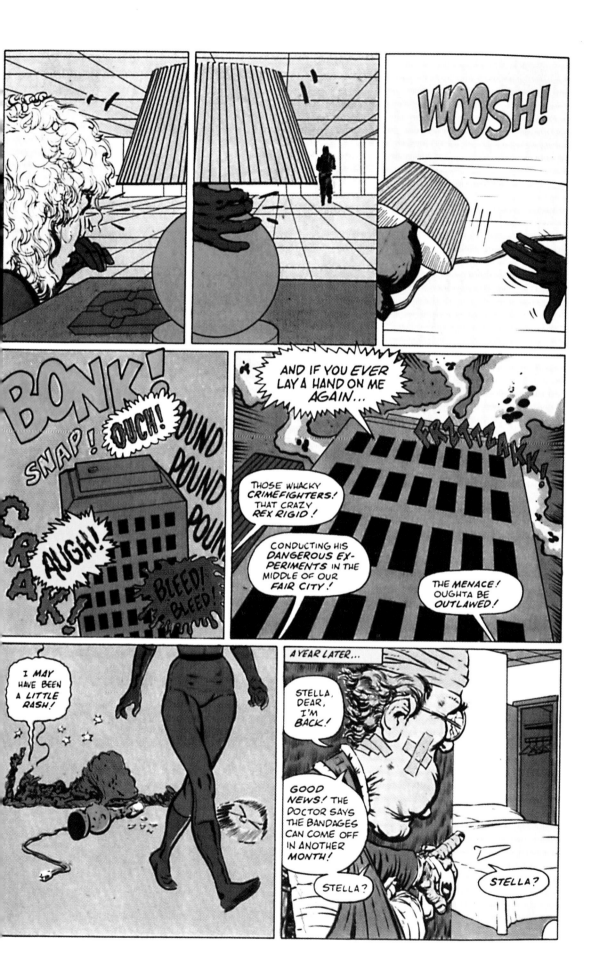

STELLA MY LOVE!

I WAS WORRIED SICK! WHEN I REALIZED WHAT I'D DONE... HOW I'D ACTED...

OH STELLA... PLEASE FORGIVE ME!

FROM NOW ON, THINGS WILL BE JUST THE WAY YOU WANT IT TO BE!

COME BACK TO THE QUAR- TET...

WE NEED YOU!

YOU'RE SO UNPROTECTED, SO UNSHELTERED OUT HERE...

YOU! WHAT ARE YOU DOING...

THE REVISIONIST HISTORIAN IS BACK IN THIS DIMENSION FOR THE FIRST TIME!

THE FATE OF THE EARTH HANGS IN THE BALANCE!

REX! SEND ME ON THE TIME TURNTABLE INTO THE DISTANT PAST!

I DON'T THINK THAT'S SUCH A GOOD IDEA...

THE TIME TURNTABLE? OF COURSE, MY OLD FRIEND! AS A MATTER OF FACT, I'VE JUST COMPLETED SOME EXPERIMENTAL ADJUSTMENTS...!

HA HA HA HA HA HA

DAT *CUTS* IT, SQUISHO! DAT WUZ MY *HERO* YOU JUST COLD-BLOODEDLY ATOMIZED! WHY, I OUGHTA--

NONSENSE, BING, OLD FRIEND! MY MODIFICATIONS WORKED *PERFECTLY!* --MEGATON MAN IS IN THE *DISTANT PAST!*

OH YEAH? WELL, IF DIS *CRAZY GIZMO* REALLY WORKS, DEN HE SHOULD BE BACK ANY *SECOND!* SO WHERE IS HE, HUH? HUH?!!!

?!!!

GOLLY! DAT *CRAZY GIZMO* REALLY *WORKS!*

WOO!

YEAH, WELL, HOW DO WE KNOW THIS IS THE *REAL* MEGATON MAN YOU BROUGHT BACK FROM THE *DISTANT PAST,* AND NOT SOME *CRUMMY IMPOSTER,* HUH?!!! HUH?!!!

PAMMY... I MEAN *STELLA*... YOUR FRIENDS SHOULD *HEAL* IN A FEW WEEKS...

I'M... I'M...

SO, I STAYED WITH THE GROUP,
BUT MY HEART JUST WASN'T
IN IT ANYMORE.

I WAS TOO WEAK, ON THE INSIDE, TO DO ANYTHING BUT HANG ON TO WHAT I HAD.

IMMEDIATELY, A STRANGE BOND WAS FORMED BE-
TWEEN THE TWO OF US, TWO PEOPLE OF VERY
DIFFERENT BACKGROUNDS...

SHE HAD ALWAYS WANTED TO WRITE A NOVEL, I HAD
ALWAYS WANTED TO GO TO COLLEGE, AND SO,
IN THAT MADHOUSE...

WE PLOTTED OUR ESCAPE...

HAHA HAHA!   HA HA HA HA!

...TO ANN ARBOR.

I SAID, "I GUESS WE'RE NEIGHBORS!" I'M KEN! REMEMBER ME?

REGISTRATION! SURE! I WAS LOST THERE FOR A MINUTE! ISN'T THIS PORCH GREAT?

WE'VE GOT LOTS IN MICHIGAN!

I HAVEN'T OWNED A PORCH SINCE I STAYED AT GRANDMA'S IN THE SUMMER AS A LITTLE GIRL...

THAT'S RIGHT, I BET YOU DIDN'T *HAVE* ONE ON THAT SKYSCRAPER.

WELL, ENJOY! SUMMER'S DYING QUICKLY!

SO YOU KNEW WHO I WAS, KEN!

THE TRANSPAREN WOMAN? NOT UNTIL JUST NOW, WHEN I SA THE CAR PARKED THERE!

HEY, I WAS MEANIN TO ASK...

I'M NOT ONE OF THOSE SUPER TYPES THAT YOU'RE USED TO, BUT I KNOW WHERE THEY STASH THE GOOD FOOD AND FILMS IN THIS TOWN! MAY I *ESCORT* YOU THIS EVENING?

HMM... YOU ARE RATHER ORDINARY...

WELL, THANKS!!!!.

NO, I MEANT THAT...

I MEANT THAT YOU'RE-- I MEAN...

YEAH! IT SOUNDS GREAT!

UNFORTUNATELY, THE "GEORGE HAS A GUN" IS SITUATED NEAR A *LARGE UNIVERSITY*, SO IT APPEARS I'LL HAVE TO SETTLE FOR BEFRIENDING STUDENTS AND FACULTY *INSTEAD*...

I'LL NEED SOME *PROPS* FOR MY *DISGUISE*...!

THESE BOOKS I *MATERIALIZE* FROM *COSMIC ETHER* SHOULD DO THE TRICK...!

I HOPE NO ONE NOTICES THAT THEY'RE PRINTED IN *ANCIENT ALPHA CENTAURIAN*, AND NOT *ENGLISH*...

HEY-- *ANCIENT ALPHA CENTAURIAN!* RIGHT?

WE CAN BEST SEE THE TWO *EXTREMES* OF *SEXUAL STEREOTYPING* IN *MEGATON MAN* AND THE *SEE-THRU-GIRL!*

ON THE ONE HAND, *MEGATON MAN*: MACHINE-LIKE, LOGICAL, UNFEELING, FEARLESS, POWERFUL, AGGRESSIVE...

ANY KIND OF *SENSITIVITY* OR *HUMANITY*, ROUTED OUT. IN A WORD: *MACHO*.

MALE

FEMALE

Fig. 9   ARTIST'S RENDERING

THEN, THERE'S THE *SEE-THRU-GIRL*: SENSUAL, PASSIVE, INDECISIVE, EMOTIONAL, CHILDLIKE... ALL THE THINGS *MEGATON MAN* IS NOT.

IN A WORD, *SEX KITTEN*.

NOW, IN REAL LIFE, NEITHER ONE OF THESE ARCHTYPES IS *REALISTIC*. WE ALL HAVE QUALITIES FROM *BOTH* EXTREMES...

HEY! SEE-THRU-GIRL! I'M IN YOUR *HUMAN SEXUALITY* CLASS, AND I THOUGHT WE COULD HELP EACH OTHER ON *HOMEWORK*...

I ADMIT, IT'S A *WEAK LINE*, EVEN FOR A *ALIEN*...

SEE-THRU GIRL?

SHHH! I'M TRYING TO KEEP A LOW *PRO-FILE!* WHO ARE YOU?

HMM... KINDA *CUTE!* HE DOESN'T *LOOK* LIKE A *MEGAHERO*...

ANTON. *ANTON DREK.* I'M UH... AN *EXCHANGE STUDENT.*

DON'T WORRY. I'M TRYING TO GO UNNOTICED FOR THE TIME BEING *MYSELF!*

HMM... KINDA *GORGEOUS*... HARD TO BELIEVE SHE'S REALLY A *MEGAHERO*...

LIKE I SAID, I'M A FOREIGN EXCHANGE STUDENT. *EXTREMELY* FOREIGN. I STUDY *NEANDERTHOL-OGY* -- THE STUDY OF *CURRENT EVENTS.* I'VE BEEN WATCHING YOU EARTHLINGS FOR *SOME TIME*... Ha Ha I MEAN, *AMERICANS*...

I'M SORRY IF I WAS RUDE TO YOU ON THE STREET MY LIFE'S BEEN GOING SO *NORMAL* LATELY, I'VE BEEN AFRAID THAT SOMETHING *WEIRD* OR *BLOCK-BUSTING* WOULD HAPPEN. *PARANOIA,* I GUESS.

BUT, THINGS HAVE BEEN PRETTY COOL. PEOPLE ARE NICE HERE.

SAY, YOU'RE THE ONLY BOY I'VE MET THAT HASN'T ASKED TO SEE MY *MEGA-POWERS* WITHIN THE FIRST *TWO MINUTES!*

MEGA-POWERS?

AND SO...

I'M SO HAPPY! YOU KNOW, IT MAY NOT SEEM LIKE MUCH TO YOU, BUT I FINALLY HAVE MY LIFE IN SOME KIND OF ORDER!

MY OWN APARTMENT, SCHOOL, A NORMAL LIFE! ITS REALLY AN ACCOMPLISHMENT!

... AND, AT LAST, A RELATIONSHIP WITH A NORMAL GUY.!!!

STELLA... I HAVE A CONFESSION TO MAKE...

I DON'T QUITE KNOW HOW TO PUT THIS...

NEXT: THE ORIGIN OF TRENT PHLOOG...

Afterword

First, let me compliment you on your good taste and discernment when it comes to color-coded sequential narratives! You've just enjoyed (hopefully) the first five issues of *Megaton Man* from the deepest, darkest 1980s. (Isn't that great? We can all relax now—ibooks has officially scraped the bottom of the barrel! Can there be any doubt that the graphic novel craze is over?)

My publisher, Byron Preiss, the originator of the graphic novel (sorry, Will!), and therefore someone keenly sensitive to getting credit for setting precedent, wants to be sure that I remind you that *Megaton Man* came out way before those watered-down rip-offs *The Tick* and *The Incredibles*. However, I think it's beneath me to disparage others who may have less personal integrity and far more lucrative merchandising than myself.

Let others chew their bubble gum and hum Monkees tunes; as far as I'm concerned, you're holding in your hands the *Sgt. Pepper's Lonely Hearts Club Band* of superhero parody. Although ultimately it is for others to say, let me humbly submit that *Megaton Man* is the real deal (after Harvey Kurtzman and Wally Wood's *Superduperman*, of course, and that *Heavy Metal* thing Berni Wrightson did).

But afterwords should look to the future, not the past, and this is a forward-looking afterword, after all. Let me be clear, my fellow Americans: in terms of *Megaton Man*, there's plenty more where this came from! That's right—more forgotten reprints, and possibly even some new stuff from the ol' drawing board! But it's all up to you, so keep those cards and letters coming! Of course, if this thing doesn't sell, the "more" in this case will stay put, right where it is—buried in Megaton Man's reinforced concrete bomb shelter. Consider it my way of blaming everybody else if this 20th anniversary collection isn't the biggest pop-culture comeback since Doc Savage. (Doc who?)

Now, let's look back. Twenty years! Has it really been that long? Wasn't it only yesterday that colorists Ray Fehrenbach and Bill Poplaski were waiting for their Cel-Vinyl paints to dry on Yarn Man? Today, in the same amount of time, I can change the color scheme of Jim Kitchen's favorite woolen character twenty times over in Photoshop, and add shading and highlights, to boot. In fact, that's what I had to do in the case of Pete Poplaski's brilliant original colorings of the *Megaton Man* covers, which somehow got lost between Wisconsin and Pittsburgh. Yes, the state-of-the-art technology has changed, but the material, hopefully, has stood the test of time. (In other words, I have yet to top this stuff despite two decades of trying!)

Okay, this is starting to sound like every liner note to every CD reissue of every band that went nowhere after their last LP in 1979. Let's face it, any declaration that "The best is yet to come!" is going to sound like nothing more than wishful thinking on the way to the "oldies" circuit. Sure, I'd like to remind everyone that I'm still alive, I'm still drawing comics, I'm still "relevant" to the "scene" (whatever that is)—that I'm at the top of my game and have never been drawing better! But this isn't about me. This is about America's love affair with goofy superheroes, and a marketing opportunity that has unexpectedly presented itself because of something I call the "Al Franken fluke" and a new big-budget Pixar release. Even I know that. And I've been told if I blow it this time, I could end up in the East River.

So let me get out of here at least trying to sound gracious. First, I'd like to thank Mr. Al Franken, for asking me to participate in a very minor way in the publishing phenomenon of 2003 that was *Lies and the Lying Liars Who Tell Them: A Fair and Balanced Look at the Right* (and for allowing us to shamelessly plaster his name all over the present volume); Byron Preiss, Steve Roman, and the hordes at ibooks, who saw fit to repackage The Man of Molecules in a way that will make *Not Brand Echh* fans everywhere profoundly jealous; and to my erstwhile publisher and born-again agent Denis Kitchen, and those original Kitchen Sinkers—Pete, Bill, Jim, and Holly, who made it all happen the first time.

I'd especially like to remember the late Dave Schreiner, who I drove crazy with cassette tapes of Peter Gabriel while he was trying to edit the whole line of fabled Kitchen Sink masterpieces—*The Spirit*, *Steve Canyon*, *Death Rattle*, et al. Dave, a backwoods newspaperman in the Mark Twain mold if there ever was one, always said there was something more enduring to *Megaton Man* than mere silly fight scenes. If you found that to be true in the stories you've just read, Dave probably had something to do with it.

Finally, thank you for your support, and Make Mine Megaton!

—Don Simpson
Pittsburgh, PA
October 26, 2004

AND SO, *THE SEE-THRU GIRL* AND *MEGATON MAN* GO ON PATROL...